WORD TRAVELERS

AND THE TAJ MAHAL MYSTERY

WORD TRAVELERS

AND THE TAJ MAHAL MYSTERY

RAJ HALDAR

ILLUSTRATED BY NEHA RAWAT

Cover and internal illustrations by Neha Rawat
Cover design by Maryn Arreguín/Sourcebooks
Internal design by Jillian Rahn/Sourcebooks

Published by Sourcebooks eXplore, an imprint of Sourcebooks Kids
P.O. Box 4410, Naperville, Illinois 60567-4410
(630) 961-3900
sourcebookskids.com

The Library of Congress Cataloging-in-Publication Data is on file with the publisher.

Source of Production: Sheridan Books, Chelsea, Michigan, United States of America
Date of Production: August 2021
Run Number: 5022545

Printed and bound in the United States of America.
SB 10 9 8 7 6 5 4 3 2 1

Have you ever wondered where the words we use every day came from? In the Word Travelers series, discover the fascinating origins of the words in **bold** using the glossary at the end of this book.

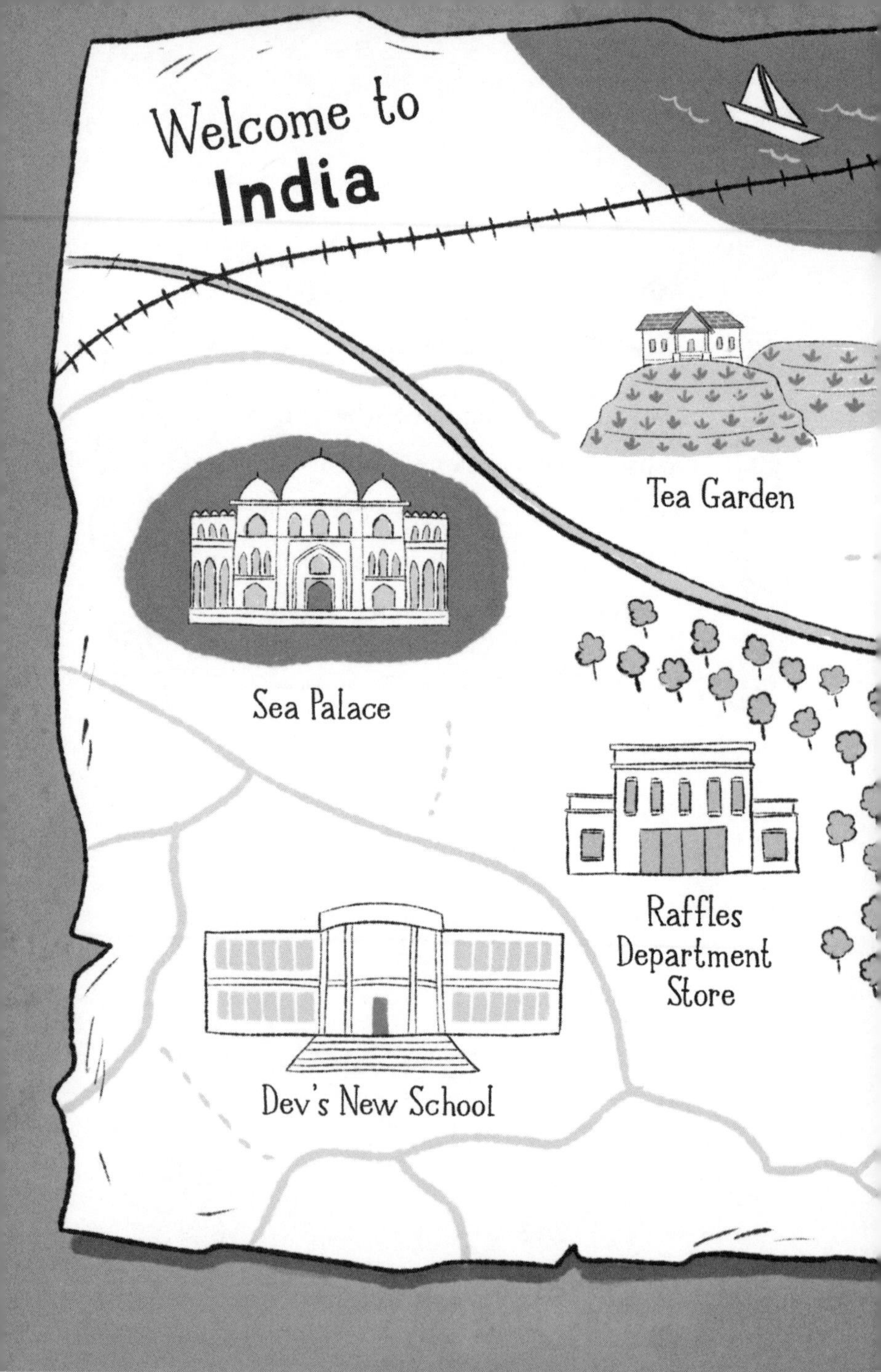
Welcome to
India
Tea Garden
Sea Palace
Raffles
Department
Store
Dev's New School

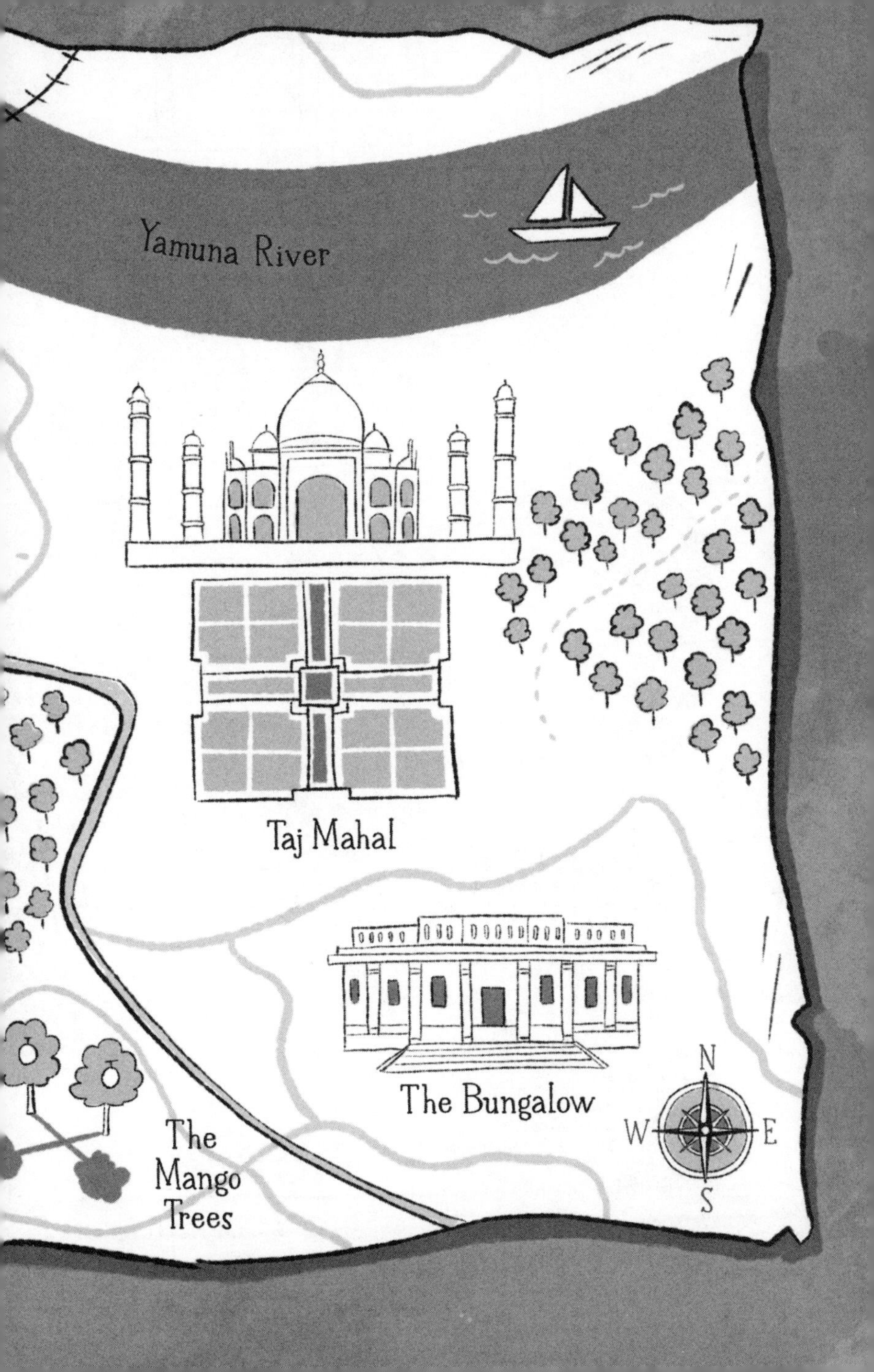

Yamuna River
Taj Mahal
The Bungalow
N
W
E
S
The Mango Trees

SUPER SATURDAY

Eddie jumped out of bed as soon as the sun came up. He ran to the bedroom window and grabbed his end of the tin-can telephone, connected by string all the way to his best friend Molly-Jean's house next door. He shouted into the empty soup can, "Are you there? Do you read me, MJ?" Eddie put the can up to his ear and waited for a response.

Finally, MJ's crackly voice came through from

the other end of the line. "What are you doing up so early?" she asked, sounding tired.

"Don't you know what today is?" Eddie replied.

MJ rubbed her eyes and looked at the calendar on her bedroom wall. "Super Saturday!" she shouted. "I'll be ready in a flash!"

For as long as Eddie and MJ could remember, Saturdays meant having a sleepover party at one of their houses. They'd play outside all day—airplane spotting (MJ's favorite) or digging for arrowheads

and other archaeological treasures in the backyard (Eddie's favorite—so far, he had found two arrowheads and four bottle caps). On rainy days they'd create obstacle courses for MJ's newts or cook up a gigantic feast while pretending to be contestants on one of those TV baking shows. After dinner, they liked to work on MJ's crossword puzzle books and stay up way past their bedtime watching some goofy old zombie movies.

While this particular Saturday started out like any other for Eddie and Molly-Jean, their evening would end up being full of surprises.

❋ ❋ ❋

It all began when Eddie's dad called out from the kitchen after dinner, "Time to get into your pajamas and brush your teeth. I promised MJ's parents that you would be asleep like *thirty minutes ago*!"

Letting out an exaggerated groan, MJ folded down the corner of the crossword puzzle they were working on to save their place, and she and Eddie dragged themselves up the stairs to get ready for bed. As they stood in the bathroom washing up, an odd question popped into Eddie's head. "What do you think the word **pajamas** means, MJ?" he asked.

She thought about it for a second while carefully scrubbing her teeth. "It's ze cloze you wear ta bed, shilly," MJ said around a mouthful of toothpaste.

"But what does the *word* really mean? Like where did it come from? Is it just a gibberish word that somebody made up?" Eddie insisted. "Pajamas, jamas, jammies, jamas," he scatted while drumming his toothbrush on the countertop.

Oh boy, thought MJ, rolling her eyes. She had just turned ten and a half years old last week, and while nine-year-old Eddie was her best bud, sometimes she felt about five years older than him.

Just then, Eddie's mom came into the bathroom, dropping off warm towels. "You'd be surprised," she said. "So many words we use every day have the most amazing stories to tell." She lowered her voice to a whisper and continued, "Go up to the attic and find the biggest, oldest book you can—it's the one my grandfather gave me when I was about your age. It was his most prized possession. You see, Eddie's great-grandpa, Oscar, was a world-famous *etymologist*—"

"What does that mean?" Eddie and MJ asked at the exact same time.

"An etymologist is someone who studies the history of words—not just what they mean, but where they came from."

"Don't words come from the dictionary?" MJ asked.

"Actually, the dictionary usually lists what words mean *now*. To understand where words come from..."

Eddie faked a snore. "C'mon mom, it's Saturday! Can you please save the school talk until Monday, at least?"

"Sure, Eddie," his mom said with a glint in her eye. "Why don't you both just head up to the attic now to find Great-Grandpa Oscar's book? He worked on it for years and years, adding thousands of words, explaining how they've come to the English language from all sorts of different places and languages. Look inside the book, and you'll find a secret story behind almost every word!

"It's a real adventure," she said with a chuckle as she walked away.

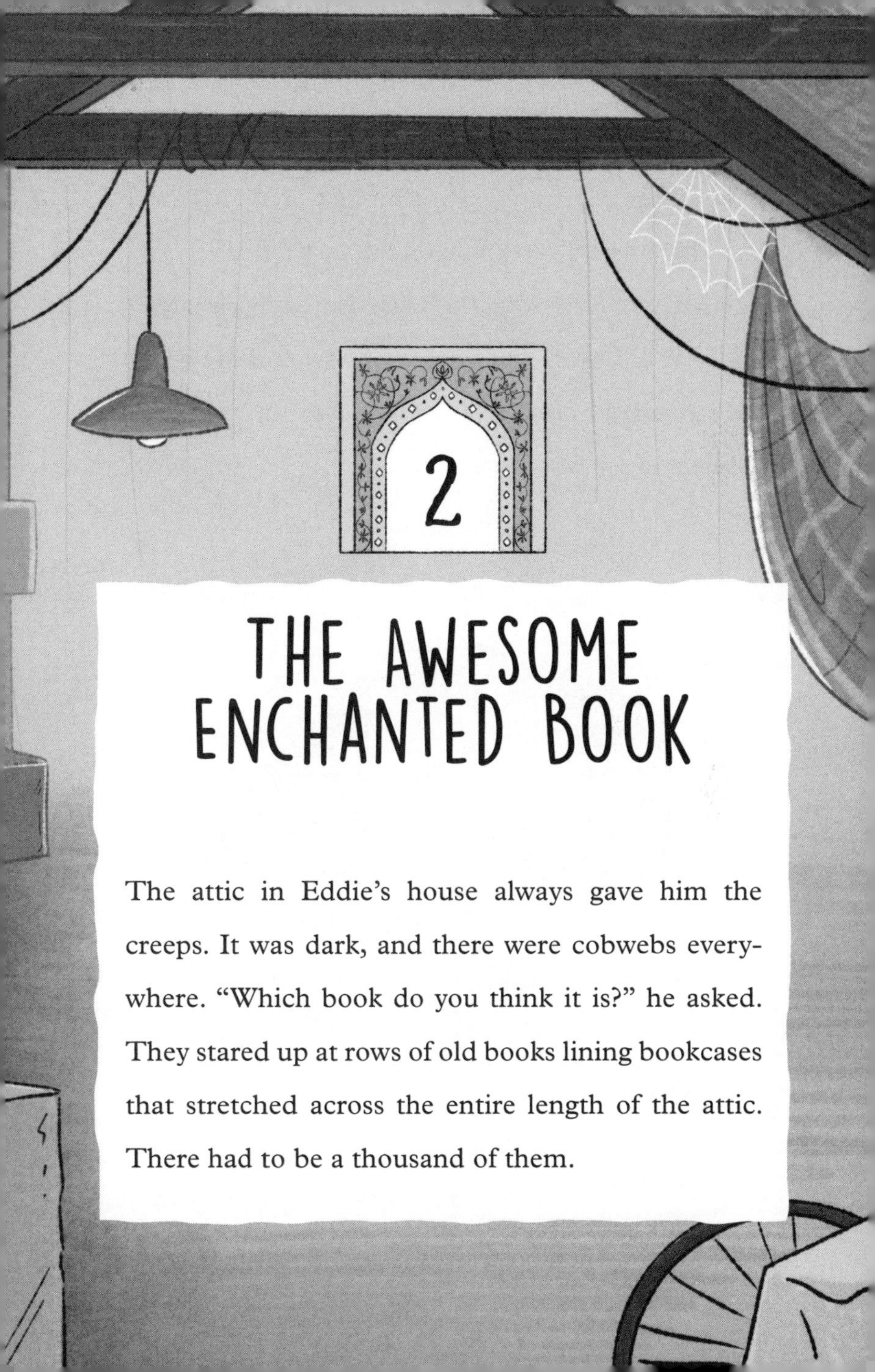

2

THE AWESOME ENCHANTED BOOK

The attic in Eddie's house always gave him the creeps. It was dark, and there were cobwebs everywhere. "Which book do you think it is?" he asked. They stared up at rows of old books lining bookcases that stretched across the entire length of the attic. There had to be a thousand of them.

"There's only one book that looks older and bigger than the rest. It must be that one!" MJ said, pointing to a worn volume on the very top shelf. The handwritten title along the spine was badly smudged and blocked by the twine wrapped around the book. MJ stretched to pull it down, but even on her tippy-toes, the book was out of her reach.

At that very moment, the book fell to the floor in front of them with a crash, the twine unraveling itself on the way. "It's like it has a mind of its own," Eddie whispered.

MJ nodded in disbelief. Moving closer to the book, Eddie bent down and blew off a thick layer of dust from the cover. Moonlight suddenly flooded the attic window, illuminating a gold globe and silver swirls of alphabet letters embossed on the book's leather cover.

"Awesome!"

"Enchanted!"

Eddie and MJ whispered together in the moonlight.

They carefully picked up the Awesome Enchanted Book and hurried downstairs to the blanket hide-away they built in Eddie's room for the sleepover. Eddie pulled out his trusty flashlight while MJ carefully pried the old book open and examined a few pages. "Every word is in order from A to Z, just like a dictionary," MJ said.

"Wait, there's a handwritten message on the first page. It must be from Great-Grandpa Oscar himself!" shouted Eddie. MJ looked again at the inside cover as Eddie read the faded note aloud:

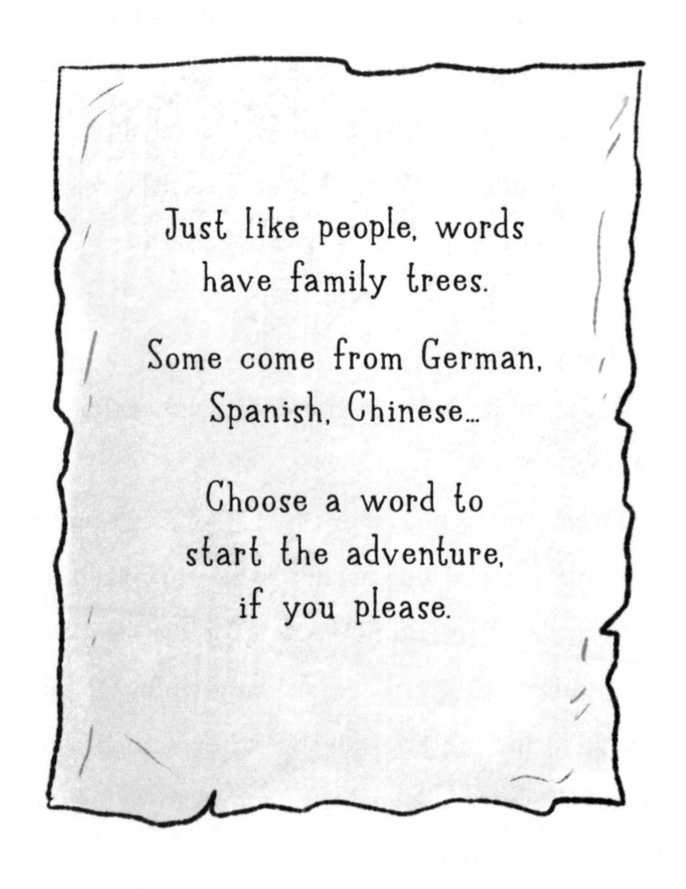

Without wasting a second, MJ flipped through the book and found the section for the letter P. "Here it is!" she exclaimed, stopping her finger right underneath the word *pajamas*.

"Well, what does it say?" Eddie asked impatiently.

"The word *pajamas* comes from India. It's made up of two smaller words: *pa*, meaning leg, and *jama*, meaning shirt."

"A shirt for your legs..." Eddie said, looking down at his own striped pajamas. "From India? I never would have guessed it!"

Suddenly, the Awesome Enchanted Book began floating above their heads, spinning faster and faster, until *poof*!—the room was filled with a swirling haze of smoke.

WHERE IN THE WORLD?

When the smoke cleared, Eddie and MJ couldn't believe their eyes. They were in a bedroom, but it definitely wasn't Eddie's bedroom, where they just were. Instead of a hideaway made with old blankets, they were sitting on a huge wooden bed with colorful silk sheets. MJ and Eddie looked at each other in amazement, noticing that their pajamas were transformed into snazzy new outfits. The Awesome Enchanted Book (or AEB, as Eddie and MJ liked to call it for short) was at their side, dust completely gone, the gold leather cover shining in the bright sunlight.

"Eddie, where in the world are we?" MJ stammered. Any time she was nervous, she tried to think about one of her all-time heroes, Mae Jemison—doctor, engineer, professor, and the first Black female astronaut. (Plus, she had the same initials as MJ!) *This wouldn't scare Mae one bit*, MJ thought as she picked up the book and gathered the courage to look around.

"Whoa! Check this out," Eddie said, pointing his finger in the direction of the bedroom window. Off in the distance, MJ saw a beautiful white building with a teardrop-shaped roof. She'd seen it before but couldn't remember where. Suddenly it came to her. "It's the Taj Mahal," she gasped. MJ recalled seeing the famous building in her family photo albums and wishing she could visit the place. "I've always wanted to take a trip here. It's where my mom's family comes from," she shouted, looking at Eddie. "We must be in India!"

Without warning, the bedroom door swung open, and a boy dressed in a crisp green tunic appeared from the hallway outside. He didn't seem to notice Eddie or MJ as he frantically tried to fit a large key into a locked closet door. Eddie decided to get his attention. "Excuse me. Is everything okay?"

The boy spun around, startled by the sound of Eddie's voice. "Oh goodness, no! Things are definitely not okay!" he cried out as he studied the duo closely. "My name is Dev. I'm the grandson of the maharaja of Jaipur."

"The maha what of where?" asked Eddie.

"Oh, you're definitely not from around here," Dev said.

"Nope," said MJ, thinking fast. "Our, um, relatives sent us here to learn more about India. I'm MJ, and this is Eddie."

"Nice to meet you, MJ and Eddie. And welcome to the city of Agra. Is this your first time here?"

Eddie, not one to get distracted by niceties, was more interested in learning about Dev's problem. "Wait, what's going on with your grandfather? And what are you doing with that key?"

Dev suddenly looked worried again. "A long time ago, my grandfather was the **maharaja**, the king who ruled this part of India. He left us a golden key hidden here in his old **bungalow**. The story goes

that the key will unlock a vast treasure passed down from generation to generation, if anyone in my family should ever need it."

Eddie and MJ looked at each other, eyes wide with excitement.

"You see," Dev continued, "a few weeks ago, a terrible storm caused flooding that ravaged our town. It rained for ten days without stopping, and the **typhoon** destroyed our school. Now, hundreds

of children have nowhere to go and learn. And it doesn't seem like our town can rebuild it anytime soon—they are focused on repairing homes, roads, and the hospital first, and I'm worried there won't be any money left after all that!"

"Wow, I'm so sorry Dev. That sounds so hard for you and your neighbors! So, you'll need to find the treasure to help fix your school?" asked MJ.

"I'm afraid so," replied Dev. "The trouble is, I've tried every door in the bungalow, and this key doesn't seem to fit any of them."

THE SECRET KEY

"Can I look at the key?" asked Eddie, hoping he might notice something that their new friend had missed. All those weekends digging for archaeological treasure in his backyard had trained Eddie to catch all the details. But, when Dev handed the key to Eddie, it slipped between his fingers and fell to the tile floor.

To everyone's surprise, the seemingly solid gold key broke in half, revealing a rolled-up piece of paper tucked inside. MJ carefully pulled out the tiny scrap of paper and discovered a message written on it.

"What could it possibly mean?" Dev wondered aloud.

"I've never heard of a shampoo that's not for hair," said Eddie.

MJ had an idea. "Why don't we look in the AEB?" They all gathered round as she opened the book—and right there, between *shadow* and *sherbet*, was *shampoo*!

"'The word **shampoo** comes from Hindi,'" Dev read. "That's one of the many languages we speak in India," he explained.

"Of course!" shouted Eddie. "It says here that

the Hindi word *champo* originally meant to press or rub, like during a massage. Over time, the word was adopted into English to describe the way we rub our hair when we wash it."

"But how does this help us with my grandfather's clue?" Dev asked.

"Hmmm..." Eddie wondered. "Shampoo...rub... rub-a-dub-dub... Try rubbing the message with your fingers, MJ!"

MJ pressed her thumbs firmly against the paper and began rubbing the words. Slowly the old message vanished, and a new one appeared. She read it aloud.

In the morning sun
At precisely nine
When the **mango**
trees align,

X marks the spot.

This time, Dev knew exactly what to do. "Whenever my grandfather went for his morning stroll, he would stop near two tall **mango** trees—"

Before he could finish, Dev was interrupted by a loud rustling sound coming from just outside the window. MJ instantly leaped into action. She poked her head out and discovered muddy footprints on the ground below next to the bushes. "I think somebody's been snooping on us," she said, looking at the others. "Hurry, we've got to find this treasure, and we don't have a second to lose!"

5

X MARKS THE SPOT

"This is where my grandfather would practice **yoga**," said Dev, pointing to a clearing beneath the two mango trees. Eddie's dad and MJ's mom took a yoga class together, so they already knew it was an ancient Indian method of relaxing your mind, while exercising your body too.

Eddie looked at his watch. "It's going to be nine o'clock in three, two..." He counted down

the seconds. Everyone was completely still, but nothing happened. "All these clues can make a *man-go* bonkers!" said Eddie, slapping his knee heartily. "Get it? *Mango?*" he repeated the joke again, looking around at his friends.

"I'm really sorry," MJ said to Dev, shaking her head. "As you can see, my best friend is a little kooky in the coconut!"

MJ decided she wanted an aerial view to see if they were missing something. Her high-flying hero, Amelia Earhart, would surely do the same. MJ pulled herself up onto a limb of one of the mango trees and looked out over the vast **jungle**. Nothing seemed out of the ordinary. Then she looked down at the clearing below, and it all made perfect sense.

At that moment, with the sun still low to the ground and rising behind the grove, the two mango

trees cast long shadows that crossed exactly in the middle like the letter X. MJ shouted, "X marks the spot!"

But Eddie couldn't hear her down below the lush green foliage. She shinnied back down the tree. "C'mon, over here!" she said, pointing toward an ordinary patch of dirt.

Without giving it a second thought, Eddie ran over and got on his hands and knees, digging with a flat

rock. "Huh…it seems like someone dug up this spot not too long ago," he said, noticing some loose soil.

MJ and Dev joined in digging too, scooping up the dirt as fast as they could. They dug until their arms were exhausted, but all they found were some aluminum scraps and a dirty yellow handkerchief with the letters G.R. stitched onto it. Eddie, loving to collect stuff, shoved the metal scraps and the handkerchief into his pocket and kept digging.

Just as they were ready to give up, Dev pointed at something shiny at the bottom of the hole they had made. He scooped out another handful of dirt and uncovered the corner of a shiny wooden box.

AN ANCIENT GAME

"It's a tea chest!" Dev exclaimed. "My grandfather used to store his tea leaves in a box just like this." As Eddie and MJ watched with excitement, Dev loosened the chest from the hole and brushed off the soil. He gently tugged the silver ring on top to remove the carved lid and passed the box to MJ.

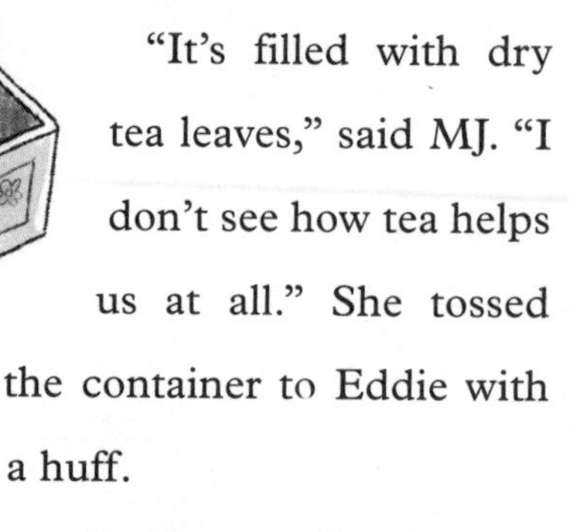

"It's filled with dry tea leaves," said MJ. "I don't see how tea helps us at all." She tossed the container to Eddie with a huff.

Feeling discouraged, Eddie turned the tea chest upside down and let its contents fall to the ground. "I guess we're back to square one," he said.

To their surprise, after the last bits of tea had been emptied from the box, a dozen torn-up pieces of paper tumbled out. "Wowie zowie!" exclaimed Eddie, using the latest catchphrase he'd learned from his dad. "Someone beat us to the next clue and then tore it to shreds. Now what are we supposed to do?"

Wait a minute, MJ thought to herself, looking at one of the bits of paper up close. "One side has an image, and the other has writing on it. The clue must have been written on the back of an old photograph.

All we have to do is put the picture together like a jigsaw puzzle, and we're back in business."

She laid the twelve scraps of paper neatly on the ground, and they got to work. Before long, an old photo of an island palace emerged, surrounded on all four sides by a gigantic lake.

"Mother once told me about this place. I think it's called Sea Palace," Dev told them. "A long time ago, my family built a beautiful summer resort on an

island at the center of a lake. Now, it's been turned into a big hotel." MJ put the last scrap of paper in place and carefully turned the entire photograph over to discover the next clue on the back.

Take a **dinghy** to
Sea Palace,

Where you must
learn the name

Of an ancient game.

Eddie scratched his head and thought for a minute. "What the heck does *dinghy* mean, and which ancient game are we supposed to play?"

In a flash, MJ picked up the AEB and flipped through the pages feverishly. "I found it! The English word **dinghy** comes from the Hindi word *dingi*, meaning small boat."

"Hurry!" Dev shouted. "There are only two

boats that leave for Sea Palace each day—one in the morning, and another precisely at four o'clock."

Eddie looked up at the afternoon sun, surprised at just how much time had passed while they had been exploring in the jungle. "If we make a dash for it now, we might still catch it!"

With that, Dev, MJ, and Eddie scurried through the dense jungle toward a clearing in the distance.

An hour later, they finally arrived at the shore of a vast lake. They were exhausted and just in time to board the last dinghy to Sea Palace. The three friends took turns rowing the small boat. When Eddie took over, MJ caught her breath and looked around. Sea Palace was nothing like the hotels she had stayed at on family vacations. Moments later, MJ found that her two friends had fallen fast asleep, so she grabbed the wooden oars and began rowing toward the island.

Just before she docked the boat, MJ nudged Eddie and Dev to wake up. They were groggy at first but quickly snapped awake at the sight of the beautiful island palace. They excitedly jumped out of the dinghy and ran to the entrance of Sea Palace. The whole place was made of white marble, and every archway had a perfect view of the sparkling blue water outside. MJ felt as though she'd stepped back in time into a royal palace from hundreds of years ago. *Incredible India*, MJ thought to herself. *And to think that my mom's side of the family comes from such a magical place.*

"How can I help you?" asked the woman at the front desk, startling MJ from her daydream.

Thinking quickly, MJ remembered the second half of the clue about the name of an ancient game and asked in her most innocent voice, "Do you have any games that my friends and I can play? Please?"

"Sure, we have plenty of board games for guests to borrow," the woman replied. "Is there one in particular I can get for you?"

Eddie butted in. "How about something that's, um, been around for a while? The dustier, the better!"

The woman chuckled and thought for a moment. "Well, the oldest board game we have is Snakes and Ladders. It's been played here in India for thousands of years."

"Wow!" Eddie, MJ, and Dev exclaimed all at once. "An ancient game."

"Funny," the woman continued, "a rather peculiar businessman just borrowed that one. As he walked away, he muttered something about a clue. But Snakes and Ladders isn't a puzzle game with clues..."

"Did you happen to get his name? So we can ask him if we can play when he is done?" Dev asked.

"Let me check my guest book," the woman said, looking down at the large binder in front of her. She brushed her finger across the page as she scanned a long list of names. Finally, she stopped on a very messy signature and peered down through her reading glasses. "It's Mr. Raffles you want to ask," she said, pointing toward a neatly dressed man with a curly mustache seated at the far corner of the lobby. "But each guest has thirty minutes with the—"

Before she could finish her sentence, Dev, MJ, and Eddie whipped around and raced toward the dapper gentleman in a gray suit at the other end of the room. He was hunched over the game board while twirling his mustache. At that very moment, having noticed Eddie, MJ, and Dev heading in his direction, Mr. Raffles quickly gathered his belongings and left.

7
THE VANISHING VILLAIN

Eddie, MJ, and Dev dashed over to the spot where the odd man had been sitting. There were game pieces scattered all over the table. “He sure left in a hurry! Pretty suspicious!” Eddie exclaimed.

“You can say that again. My mom would be peeved about a mess like this,” said MJ. She started

picking up the pieces one by one.

"I don't see any sign of our next clue here."

Just then, Eddie noticed a bright yellow notebook peeking out from underneath the table. "Property of Geoffrey Raffles," he said, picking it up and reading the words on the book's cover aloud.

"G.R.!" shouted MJ. "The initials on the handkerchief we found by the mango trees must stand for *Geoffrey Raffles*. What do you think this Mr. Raffles is up to?"

Eddie flipped through the pages of Mr. Raffles's empty diary. "No answers here. Just another dead end." He sighed.

"Not so fast!" MJ said, finding a torn edge in the front of the notebook. "It looks like there's a page missing. Mr. Raffles must have taken it with him."

Peering over MJ's shoulder, Dev noticed something too. "See how hard Mr. Raffles pushes down when he writes? I can almost make out some words pressed into the page below."

The three friends passed the book around, taking turns trying to read the message. But it was useless—the pen etchings were too light. Suddenly, MJ remembered a trick she learned in art class. "I've got a plan," she said, grabbing a pencil from a nearby table.

"This is called a rubbing," MJ explained, gently brushing the pencil across the sheet of paper in the journal. As she colored the page, Eddie and Dev were amazed to see words start to appear, clear as day. When she finished, MJ read Mr. Raffles's entire diary entry to her friends.

Dearest Edgar,

Oh, younger brother, do I have news for you! The story our father told us about the treasure is true!

All those years ago, when he was working as the maharaja's accountant, Father overheard him talking about an ancient family treasure—one that could only be found using a special golden key.

I went to their bungalow today to see if I might find the key for myself. To my surprise, the old maharaja's grandson and his friends had already beaten me to it. But I'll have the last laugh. I listened in on those clever kids as they discussed the treasure and learned of the first clue. Now, I've snatched the next two clues from right under their little noses.

If we can solve the riddle I found inside this board game, the loot will be ours—and this little plan to steal the maharaja's treasure will have worked out delightfully. Here is the clue:

Four ingredients plus tea
Gets you the real key.

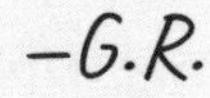

"I'm sure I've heard it before, but what does **loot** mean?" asked Eddie.

"Oh dear," cried Dev. "Loot comes from the Hindi word *lut*. It means 'stolen property.' Mr. Raffles and his brother are trying to steal my family's treasure!"

"Then we're going to get to it before he does," Eddie said, more determined than ever. He looked down at the diary again. "*Four ingredients plus tea.* I wonder what that could mean..."

Dev snapped his fingers. "There's a tea garden owned by my family not far from here. Let's go there now, before it's too late!"

A TRIP TO THE TEA GARDEN

Even though his parents usually had a cup of tea every morning, Eddie never really thought about where it came from. “The tea plants grow best in high places where it’s cool and dry,” Dev explained as they climbed the final steps to his family tea garden.

Once Eddie, MJ, and Dev reached the top of

the hill, they stopped to take in the scenery. "The view from up here is fantabulous!" said Eddie. "That means it's fantastic *and* fabulous."

"And there goes Eddie making up his own words again," said MJ, sticking her tongue out at her best friend. "One thing's for sure: this is *nothing* like our gardens at home. You call this a garden?"

The hills were lined with bright green rows of tea plants as far as the eye could see. In front of them, a beautiful house stood watch over the fields below.

As they walked toward the house, they spotted Mr. Raffles up ahead, shaking hands with someone at the front door.

"Quick! Let's go to the side window and see if we can get a better look," said Dev.

The three friends peeked through the open window into a grand room. They saw Mr. Raffles sitting at a table, while an older man wearing a pink turban showed him a variety of different teas. "My good sir," Mr. Raffles said. "Do you know of any

special drink that is made using tea and *exactly* four other ingredients?"

The old man looked up and thought for a moment. "Why, yes!" he exclaimed. "Years ago, the maharaja of Jaipur would come here on hot summer days to enjoy a glass of **punch**," the man remembered. "As you may know, *paanch* is how we say the

number five in many Indian languages," he continued. "Our recipe had five ingredients, but sadly I've forgotten what they are."

"Think, you fool!" Raffles was losing his patience.

Outside, Eddie started flipping through the AEB to find the entry for punch. MJ shook her head and whispered, "Mr. Raffles is something else. If we weren't spying on him right now, I'd march in there and give him a punch myself!"

Hearing a loud thud, the children looked back inside and saw the old man place a giant recipe book on the table. He flipped through the book furiously and stopped on a page that showed a tall glass filled with juice. "I've found it! Our punch is made with these five ingredients—water, lemon,

herbs, fruit, and tea. But, what's this? There's something else scribbled on the corner of the page..."

As the man leaned closer, to try and read the recipe, Raffles reached out and tore the whole page from the book. He looked down for a moment and suddenly sprang up from his seat. "I must leave immediately," he announced, stuffing the piece of paper into his coat pocket as he sprinted toward the door.

Before the poor old man could say anything, Mr. Raffles was gone.

9 FOLLOW THAT MAN!

Eddie, MJ, and Dev followed Raffles all the way from the hilltop tea plantation down to the bustling town in the valley below. “He’s getting away!” cried MJ, seeing Raffles pull away in a tiny, three-wheeled taxicab called an auto-rickshaw.

The three kids jumped into the next available

auto-rickshaw. "Follow that man!" Eddie told the driver, and they shot off into the busy street like a rocket.

MJ was nearly done explaining Mr. Raffles's wrongdoings to their driver when their vehicle came to a sudden stop. MJ poked her head out the window and saw a long line of cars and trucks waiting quietly in front of them.

"**Holy cow!**" exclaimed Eddie.

The driver turned around and said, “That’s exactly right, young man. In many cultures and religions, people believe cows are holy. And throughout India, people treat cows in that way. You see, there’s one sitting in the street up ahead,” he continued. “Instead of honking our horns, we will patiently wait until she decides to move.”

“But Mr. Raffles is getting away!” cried Dev, watching as the wily businessman stepped out of his auto-rickshaw up ahead.

“Well, what are you waiting for?” asked the driver. “This ride is on me. Go get him!”

The kids thanked the kind driver and jumped out of the auto-rickshaw, grabbing the trusty old AEB from the seat as they left. “Look!” said MJ with amazement. “The Taj Mahal is just ahead. That’s where Mr. Raffles must be going!”

And the three friends gave chase.

INSIDE THE TAJ MAHAL

Mr. Raffles was pacing back and forth at the entrance to the Taj Mahal. As they raced toward him, MJ looked up and understood why everyone called it the world's most famous building. "It's perfect!" she exclaimed.

Just then, Raffles noticed the kids sprinting in

his direction. He immediately crumpled up the clue from the recipe book and tossed it into the long reflecting pool in front of the Taj Mahal.

"I won't be needing that anymore," he said, letting out a wheezy chuckle. "There's no stopping me now! I'll beat you kids to the treasure, so Edgar and I can finally turn your wretched school into a shopping mall." With that, he turned around and stepped through the huge white archway and into the Taj Mahal.

"So that's why he wants to get his hands on the treasure," said Eddie. "If he gets to it first, we won't be able to fix the school, and the greedy Raffles brothers can build their shopping mall right in the center of town instead."

"Not if I've got anything to do with it," said MJ as she marched through the entrance. "Come on!"

"This is even more spectacular than the outside," said Eddie, following his friend inside. Their footsteps echoed throughout the cavernous space, with towering columns holding up archways, all wrought out of intricately carved marble, crystals, and gems.

Just then, they heard Raffles's voice from the other side of the room. He repeated the clue from the recipe book to himself, not knowing that Dev, Eddie, and MJ could hear his voice ricochet through the archways, loud and clear.

In the Taj Mahal,

Start with an
animal's name.

From another land it came:

Mongoose, Cheetah,
Tiger, or Jackal.

Dev nudged his two friends and motioned toward a patch of gray tiles on the wall nearest to them.

"Good eye, Dev! Each of those tiles has a picture of one of the animals from the clue," whispered MJ.

Staring at the tiles, Dev repeated the second part of the riddle, "*From another land it came...* But we find each of these animals here in India."

"Maybe it's not about the animals themselves," said Eddie as he carefully opened the AEB. "Maybe your grandfather is asking us which animal's *name* doesn't come from an Indian word."

"Well done, Eddie! Now you're thinking like *your* grandfather!" MJ said.

"Let me see. *Tiger* must be an Indian word, because it's our national animal," explained Dev.

They gathered around the AEB as Eddie looked up the other words one by one. "**Cheetah** comes from a Hindi word that means 'spotted,'" he whispered. The kids heard Mr. Raffles's footsteps getting closer. Eddie flipped as quickly as he could to the M section and found the next animal. "Here we go! **Mongoose** comes from an Indian word too. It means 'snake killer.'" He shaped his hand into a snake's head and made a slithering sound.

The kids looked up and saw Raffles heading toward them from across the large room. "There's no time to goof around," grumbled MJ, grabbing the book from Eddie. But when she found the final word, **jackal**, MJ could hardly believe her eyes. "Something must be wrong here," she hurriedly told the others. "It says that 'jackal' comes from a word meaning 'howler' in the ancient Indian language of Sanskrit."

"So all four of the animal names come from Indian words?" Eddie asked. "What the heck are we supposed to do now?" For the first time in their big adventure, Eddie and MJ were fresh out of ideas.

Just then, Dev picked up the Awesome Enchanted Book and it magically opened on its own to the exact page with the entry for *tiger.* "Of course!" cried Dev, reading aloud. "Although it is the national animal of India, the word actually comes from French—"

All of a sudden it was completely quiet inside the cavernous Taj Mahal as Mr. Raffles's footsteps fell silent. "Where did he go?" Dev whispered.

"I don't know, but I'm not waiting to find out!" Eddie replied as he leaped up and pressed his palm against the tile with the tiger on it. The kids heard a rumbling sound and, just like that, the solid wall in front of them opened to reveal a secret chamber.

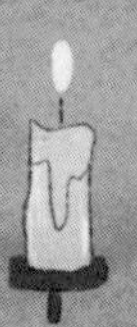

11

A SECRET PASSAGEWAY

"My grandfather spoke about secret tunnels and rooms in the Taj Mahal," said Dev as he led Eddie and MJ down a long candlelit hallway. "The Taj Mahal was built a long time ago by the emperor Shah Jahan, in memory of his beautiful wife, Mumtaz," he continued, remembering his grandfather's words. "It took twenty thousand people more than twenty years to complete, and it is said that some of those workers built secret passageways and rooms behind the white marble that covers the outside of the Taj Mahal."

When they finally reached the end of the hallway, Eddie and MJ found themselves facing an enormous stone wall.

"And here we are at another dead end," MJ said.

"Wait a second," Eddie said, noticing some writing on the stone tiles that made up the center of the wall.

At that moment, Mr. Raffles stepped out from behind the shadows at the far end of the hallway. He had been following the kids all along. Eddie looked down and saw that Raffles was barefoot. "You took your shoes off so we couldn't hear your footsteps!" Eddie exclaimed.

"I must admit, you're smarter than I thought," said Raffles, leaning casually against the wall as he put his shoes back on. "Don't mind me. I'll just wait here while you children do all the work, and then I'll take the treasure for myself!"

"You'll do no such thing," snapped MJ, turning her back on Mr. Raffles to inspect the clue on the wall. "I've seen something like this before in my puzzle books," she whispered. "It's an anagram."

"Ana-*who*?" asked Eddie.

"It's just another name for a word jumble. We have to rearrange the letters to find the answer."

"Mere cash, mere cash, mere cash..." Eddie said to himself until the words lost their meaning. Then it hit him—"**Cashmere**! The first word is cashmere. That's what our moms call their wool scarves, right MJ?"

"Very clever," said Mr. Raffles. "Yes, it is indeed a woolen scarf, or anything that's made of wool from the cashmere goat. The name comes from an old spelling of the mountain region of Kashmir in the northern part of India!"

MJ moved the tiles around to rearrange the letters in the first part of the clue. "There we go!" she said, sliding the last letter into place. Everyone was silent, but nothing happened.

Looking at the second part of the clue, Eddie was totally baffled. "It's useless," he said. "There's no way we're going to figure this one out. We're stuck!"

Suddenly, Mr. Raffles snatched the Awesome Enchanted Book from MJ and held it up to the light. "This book of yours must have the answer," he said, trying with all his might to open it. But the book wouldn't budge for Mr. Raffles, staying firmly closed. Instead, it catapulted itself in the air and fell to the floor, open at MJ's feet. As she picked it up, MJ just happened to catch the words *blue jeans* right there on the page.

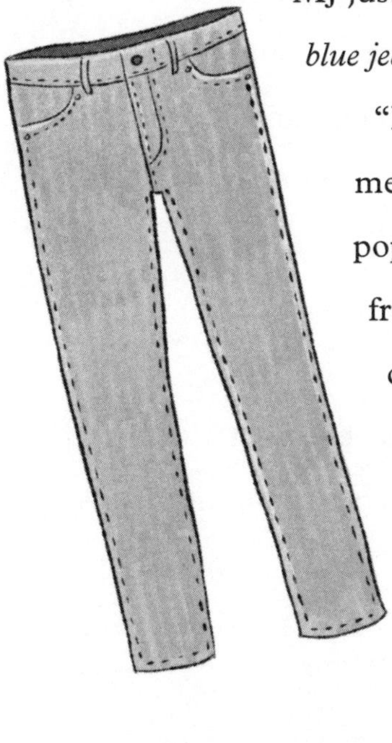

"It says here that **dungaree** means jeans, the blue trousers, popular around the world, made from denim. And that the word dungaree comes from the Hindi word *dungri*, which is a thick, blue cotton cloth," MJ explained.

Eddie knew exactly what to do. He began moving the letters in *underage* around. Eddie slid the letter D up to the front, moved the U into the second position, and kept going. "There! Now it says *dungaree*," he said as he set the last letter into place.

Without warning, the whole room began to shake. It felt almost like the earthquakes Eddie and MJ heard about on the TV news. Looking down, Dev saw two impossibly heavy stones coming free from the wall in front of them to reveal a small passageway, only big enough for kids to wriggle into.

Raffles tried to make a dash for it. "Hurry!" Eddie yelled. The trio got on their hands and knees and began squeezing into the tiny opening. With MJ and Dev in front of him, Eddie felt the brush of a hand as he crawled inside, just out of Mr. Raffles's reach.

"I guess your grandfather's clue was right," said Eddie. "You *do* have to be underage to fit inside this teeny tunnel!"

The kids crept deeper into the passageway. After a while, Dev called out to the others, "I don't know about this..." The farther they went, the darker and tighter the tunnel became.

"Do you think we should turn around?" asked Eddie. He was starting to feel dizzy in the pitch-black space.

Just then, a glint of light caught MJ's eye. "Look down there," she called. "That must be the way out!" As they got closer, she felt a refreshing draft of cool air coming from the opening up ahead.

After carefully lowering themselves through a small opening on the floor of the tunnel, Eddie, MJ, and Dev were speechless as they gazed out at a vast treasure room. There were piles of gold coins, precious gems, and ancient Indian artifacts everywhere. The three friends turned and smiled at one another, basking in the room's golden glow.

12 THE SPARKLING NEW SCHOOL

With such an immense treasure at his disposal, Dev would have his sparkling new school ready in no time, so he and his classmates could return to class. He even asked Eddie and MJ to help him draw up the plans alongside the team of architects and engineers.

Not only did they furnish each classroom

with brand-new desks, books, and a computer for every student, but Eddie and MJ had some unusual suggestions: The new school would have an observatory with an enormous telescope for peering into space; a new library named the Awesome Enchanted Library, with books on every subject, and an extra-large collection of books about etymology; and a conference room with a giant projector so Dev and his friends could video chat with Eddie and MJ's school classes whenever they wanted to.

What they were most excited about was the gigantic new playground they designed, with a zipline, two-story racing slides, and a giant trampoline. At the center of it all, MJ and Eddie requested to add a carousel featuring Indian elephants and tigers.

"I don't know how to thank you," Dev said to Eddie and MJ as they strolled the grounds at the ribbon-cutting ceremony on the first day at the new school.

"We're the ones who should be thanking you," MJ replied. "This has been an epic adventure, and we learned that so many words we use all the time come from India! How's that for a souvenir, Eddie? We can take some new words with us!"

"Let me give you each an actual souvenir as a token of my gratitude," said Dev as he reached into his pocket. He handed MJ a beautiful golden **bangle** and offered Eddie a bright indigo **bandanna** printed with swirling shapes.

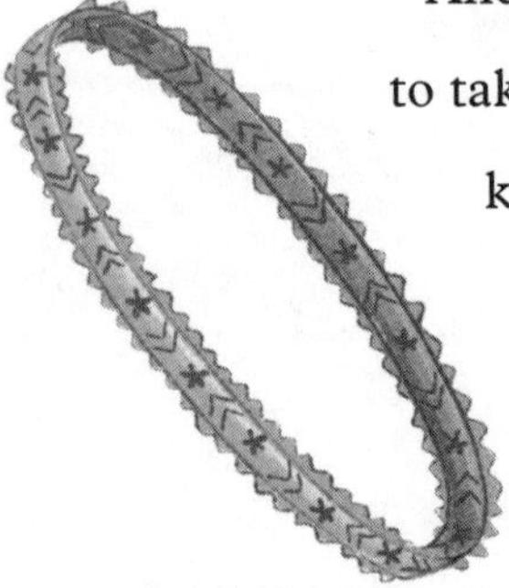

"And here's one more word souvenir to take with you, my friends. Did you know that *bandanna* comes from a Hindi word that means 'to tie'?" Dev asked, winking at his friends.

Suddenly, the kids noticed Mr. Raffles and his brother, Edgar, off in the distance, surrounded by a crowd of onlookers. "What are *they* doing here?" Eddie asked suspiciously.

"It turns out that having a shiny new school in town is going to make those unscrupulous brothers even richer," sighed Dev. "You see, business is booming at the Raffles Department Store on the other side of town—with notebooks, backpacks, and other school supplies flying off the shelves in preparation for the new school opening."

"So, that's why they're here shaking hands with everyone at the ceremony," said Eddie. "After trying to steal the treasure to build a shopping mall on this land, the rotten Raffles brothers are acting like it was their idea to fix the school all along."

"Next time we cross paths, I'm going to teach

those old dogs a few new tricks," MJ said, placing her hands firmly on her hips. "For now, though, like one of my all-time heroes, Amelia Earhart, used to say, 'all okay!'"

The second MJ uttered those words, the Awesome Enchanted Book once again began floating in the air, spinning faster and faster until—*poof*!

OUR LITTLE SECRET

"It's ten o'clock in the morning, and your blueberry pancakes are getting cold!" Eddie's mom shouted from the bottom of the stairs.

The kids were back home in their pillow fort wearing their pajamas, the Awesome Enchanted Book sitting on the floor in front of them. They

looked at each other with astonishment and walked out of the bedroom in a daze.

It wasn't until after they'd brushed their teeth and eaten breakfast that Eddie and MJ finally went back upstairs to clean up the blankets and pillows strewn about Eddie's bedroom. "Is there something under your pillow too?" MJ whispered. Eddie slowly nodded his head.

For a moment, Eddie and MJ stared in disbelief at the indigo bandanna and glittering bangle. India felt so close, right there in their hands.

At last, the silence was broken by the familiar

sound of Eddie's younger sister racing her bicycle down the sidewalk with her friends. Eddie picked up the Awesome Enchanted Book, and MJ tied a shoelace tightly around the cover. They carefully slid it into the top drawer of Eddie's dresser.

Would they untie that shoelace and open the book again? Would there be more word stories to uncover? Well, of course! But on this Sunday morning, MJ had to go finish her math homework, and Eddie had to go help his mom rake the yard.

"Don't forget your pajamas!" Eddie reminded MJ with a wink as she packed up her backpack.

"Never ever!" MJ said as she walked out the door.

GLOSSARY
OF WORD ORIGINS

Bandanna

(n.) ban-ˈda-nə

A large handkerchief, typically having a colorful pattern, worn tied around the head or neck. It comes from the Hindi word *bandhana*, meaning "to tie or fasten."

Bangle

(n.) ˈbaŋ-gəl

An ornamental ring worn on the arm or ankle. It comes from the Hindi word *bangri*, meaning "colored glass bracelet or anklet."

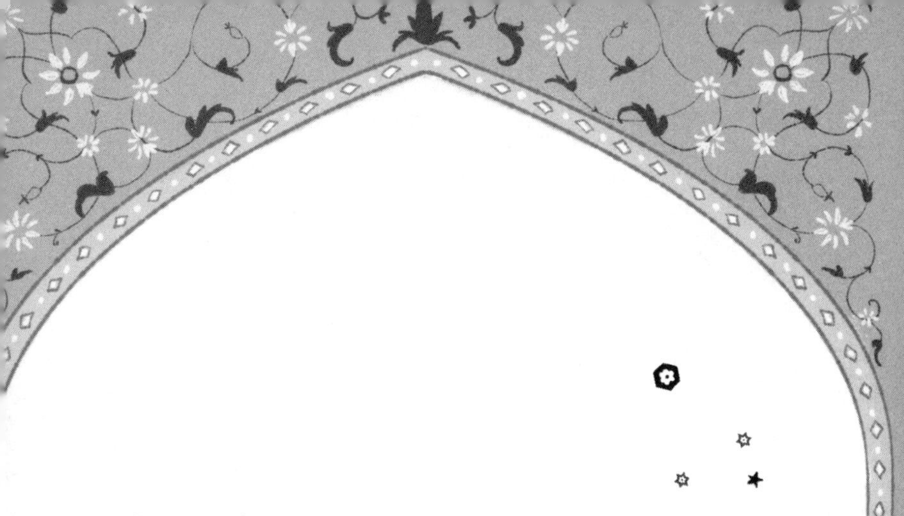

Bungalow

(n.) ˈbəŋ-gə-ˌlō

A low house, with a broad front porch, having either no upper floor or upper rooms set in the roof. It comes from the Hindi word *bangla*, meaning "belonging to Bengal."

Cashmere

(n.) ˈkazh-ˌmir

Fine, soft wool typically used for scarves and shawls. It comes from the old spelling of Kashmir, a kingdom in the Himalayan mountain range where wool was obtained from long-haired goats.

Cheetah

(n.) ˈchē-tə

A large spotted cat found in parts of Asia and Africa. It is the fastest animal on land. It comes from the Hindi word *chita*, meaning "spotted or distinctively marked."

Dinghy

(n.) ˈdiŋ-ē

A small boat for recreation or racing, especially an open boat with a mast and sails. It comes from the Hindi word *dingi*, meaning "small boat."

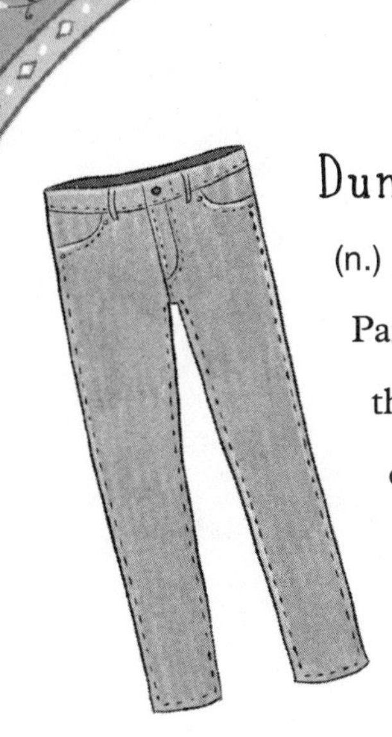

Dungaree

(n.) ˌdəŋ-gə-ˈrē

Pants made of blue jeans material, a thick, cotton cloth called "denim." It comes from the Hindi word *dungri*, meaning "coarse calico," in turn from the name of a village, now one of the quarters of the city of Mumbai.

Holy cow!

(expression) ˈhō-lē ˈkau̇

An exclamation of surprise used mostly in the United States, Canada, Australia, and England. The expression is partially based on the honor shown to cows in Hinduism.

Jackal

(n.) ˈja-kəl

A slender, long-legged wild dog found in South Asia and Africa. It comes from the word *srgala* in the ancient Indian language of Sanskrit, meaning "the one who howls."

Jungle

(n.) ˈjəŋ-gəl

An area of land overgrown with dense forest vegetation, typically in the tropics. It comes from the word *jangal* in the ancient Indian language of Sanskrit, meaning "rough and arid terrain."

Loot

(n.) ˈlüt

Stolen goods or property. It comes from the Hindi word *lut*, meaning "stolen property."

Maharaja

(n.) ˌmä-hə-ˈrä-jə

An Indian title meaning "king" or "great ruler." For hundreds of years, they ruled kingdoms all over the country of India.

Mango

(n.) ˈmaŋ-(ˌ)gō

A fleshy yellowish-red tropical fruit that is eaten ripe or used green for pickles and chutney. It comes from the word *mankay* in the Tamil language of South India, meaning "mango tree fruit."

Mongoose

(n.) ˈmän-ˌgüs

A small mammal with a long body and tail, native to Asia and Africa. It comes from the word *mangus* in the Mahrathi language of India, meaning "snake killer."

Pajama

(n.) pə-ˈjä-mə

A suit of loose pants and jacket or shirt for sleeping in. It comes from the Hindi word *pajama*, made up of two smaller words: *pa*, meaning leg, and *jama*, meaning shirt.

Punch

(n.) ˈpənch

Punch is the term for a wide assortment of drinks, generally containing fruit or fruit juice. It comes from the Sanskrit word *paanch*, meaning “five,” as the drink was originally made with five ingredients.

Shampoo

(n.) sham-ˈpü

A liquid mixture containing detergent or soap for washing hair. It comes from the Hindi word *champo*, meaning “to press or knead.”

Typhoon

(n.) tī-ˈfün

A tropical storm in the region of the Indian or western Pacific Oceans. It comes from the Hindi word *tufan*, meaning big cyclonic storm.

Yoga

(n.) ˈyō-gə

A spiritual discipline that includes breath control, meditation, and the adoption of specific bodily postures. It comes from the word *yoga* in the ancient Indian language of Sanskrit, meaning "union."

ACKNOWLEDGMENTS

This book would not have been possible without the hard work of so many brilliant folks. When Word Travelers was just an idea in my head, rock star educator and friend Alycia Zimmerman was so invaluable to the early process of figuring out how to explain difficult concepts about etymology in a way that kids would not only grasp but find truly fascinating. I could never overemphasize how important a role my editor, Kelly Barrales-Saylor, has played in bringing the series to life. To my wife, Amrita, whose genius I'm very lucky to have at my disposal whenever I need it (all too often!). And to my team:

Cathy, Bridget, Peter, and Jade, who never hesitate to come along for every new quixotic (cool etymology alert!) adventure with me.

ABOUT THE AUTHOR

Raj Haldar must like words a lot. Under his alter ego, Lushlife, as the rapper and multi-instrumentalist, he's spent close to a decade fitting words together into remarkable rhymes for fans all over the world. So it should come as no surprise that Raj's children's books are all about words too. His first picture book series, which includes *P Is for Pterodactyl*, was an instant smash with word nerds of all ages who love having fun with silent letters, homonyms, and other hilariously confusing parts of the English language. Now, with the Word Travelers series, Raj is introducing kids to the fascinating world of etymology and word origins, following his heroes Eddie and Molly-Jean on their globe-trotting adventures to discover how common words came into the English language from cultures around the world.

ABOUT THE ILLUSTRATOR

Neha Rawat is a children's book illustrator from India and a grand prize winner of the SCBWI Summer Spectacular Portfolio Showcase 2020.

She worked as a software engineer for five years before freelancing as an artist and creating custom illustrations, comics, and merchandise before eventually moving to children's books.

In her spare time, Neha can be found petting, booping and belly-rubbing dogs.

Connect with her on Instagram @nrbstudio.in.

FOLLOW EDDIE AND MJ ON THEIR NEXT ADVENTURE!

COMING JANUARY 2022